George and Bungle look very hard. They look everywhere in the cupboard. They cannot find the badge.

"I'm sure it's here somewhere," says Bungle.

They look again. They look high and low. They look here there and everywhere. Bungle's sunshine badge is nowhere to be seen. It cannot be found.

George and Bungle sit down and wonder what to do. George has an idea.

"You can borrow my sunshine badge," he says. "It's on the shelf."

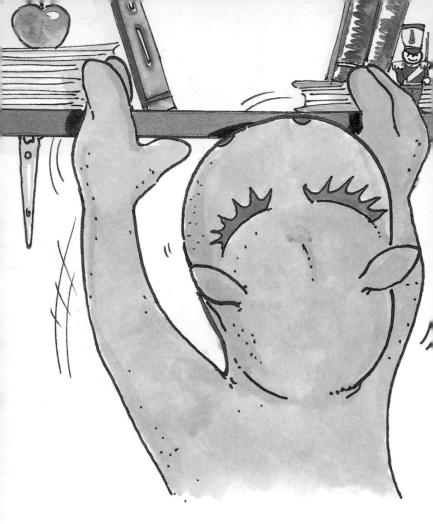

George looks on the shelf. The badge is not there. He looks on another shelf. It isn't there either. It isn't on any of the shelves.

Zippy comes in. The room is now very untidy.

"What are you doing?" he asks.

"We're looking for our sunshine badges," says Bungle.

"Come and help us look," says Bungle.

"There's no need," says Zippy. "I have a sunshine badge too. You can borrow mine.

"Thank you, Zippy," says Bungle. "Where is it?"

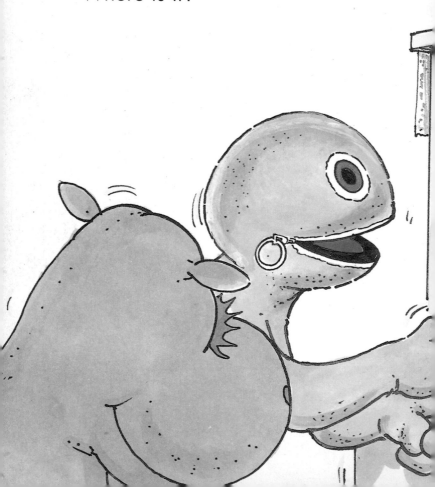

"It's in the chest of drawers," says Zippy. He goes over and opens the bottom drawer.

Zippy looks inside the drawer. He moves things about. He takes things out. He looks everywhere in the drawer. The badge is not there.

Zippy looks inside the next drawer. He moves things about. He takes things out. He looks everywhere, but he doesn't find the badge.

"Can't you find yours either?" asks George.

"I know it's in these drawers somewhere," says Zippy.

"Perhaps it's in the next one," says Bungle. "Let's look.

They all look inside the drawer.
They cannot find the badge.
    "Let's try the next one," says
George.
    The badge is not there.

Bungle and George cannot find their badges. And Zippy can't find his badge either.

"They must be in this room somewhere," says Bungle.

"I agree," says Zippy. "They can't have got up and walked away. They have to be in here somewhere."

"Let's look everywhere then," says George.

Zippy, George and Bungle search the room. They look under this. They look behind that. They look inside this. They empty that. Soon the room is full of things.

There are things on the floor. There are things on the beds. The drawers and cupboards are open. There are things all over the place.

They still cannot find the badge.
The room is a mess. Geoffrey
comes in. He sees how untidy the
room is.

"What a good idea," he says.

Zippy, George and Bungle are puzzled. The room is in a mess and yet Geoffrey is smiling.

"A good idea?" says Bungle, surprised.

"Yes," says Geoffrey. "It's time we had a spring clean."

George does not understand. "We haven't got any springs to clean, Geoffrey."

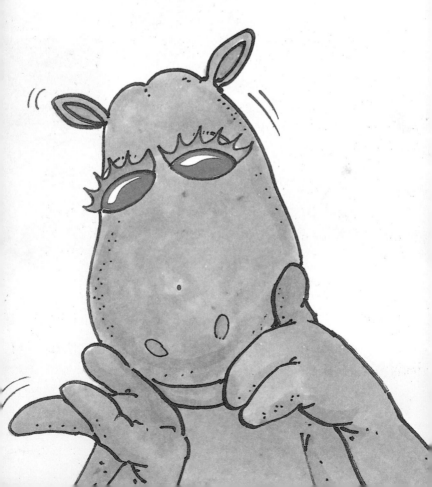

Geoffrey laughs. "To 'spring clean' means to take everything out and give it a good clean. You throw away things you don't need. Then you put things back neat and tidy."

Geoffrey gives Zippy, George and Bungle a hand. They take everything out. They clean inside the cupboards and drawers. They throw away what they don't need.

Bungle finds his badge. Then George finds his badge. Then Zippy finds his badge too! They put everything back neat and tidy.

"Everything is much easier to find when you spring clean!" laughs George.